Larry Gets Lost in San Diego

Illustrated by John Skewes
Written by Eric Ode and John Skewes

little bigfoot
an imprint of sasquatch books
seattle, wa

For Chuck, Sandie, and Connor: the original Pete

Manufactured in China by C&C Offset Printing Co. Ltd. Shenzhen, Guangdong Province, in June 2017

Published by Little Bigfoot, an imprint of Sasquatch Books

21 20 19 18 17   9 8 7 6 5 4 3 2 1

Editor: Christy Cox
Production editor: Em Gale
Design: Mint Design

Library of Congress Cataloging-in-Publication Data is available.

ISBN: 978-1-63217-121-4

Sasquatch Books
1904 Third Avenue, Suite 710
Seattle, WA 98101
(206) 467-4300
www.sasquatchbooks.com
custserv@sasquatchbooks.com

This is **Larry.** This is **Pete.**
They're friends through and through.

They plan, and they build,
and they make something new.
Then Dad says, "Come on!
We have things left to do!"

LEGOLAND
Piece by piece, brick by brick. It took more than fifty-seven million Legos to build the twenty-two thousand sculptures in California's Legoland. The park also features exciting rides, a water park, and the creature-filled Sea Life Aquarium.

LA JOLLA CHILDREN'S POOL
What strange-looking children! In 1932 a seawall was built to create a safe swimming area for kids. It also created a perfect home for sea lions and harbor seals. You can still use the beach, but stay back and give the seals lots of room.

They find people soaring
from colorful sails
and wet, whiskered creatures
with flippers and tails.

Then they hop in the car,
and they're soon on their way,
up, over a bridge
as it crosses a bay.

Old Point Loma Lighthouse

Point Loma

Pacific Ocean

Hotel del Coronado

Coro...

BIRTHPLACE OF CALIFORNIA
Because it was the first site Europeans
settled on the Pacific coast, San Diego
is sometimes called "the birthplace of
California." But Native Americans had been
living here for more than ten thousand years.

A lighthouse, a sailboat—
Pete flashes a grin,
while Larry waits wondering
where they'll begin.

They come to a busy
and fancy hotel
with new things to hear
and to see and to smell.

But Larry finds one smell . . .

HOTEL DEL CORONADO
When it was built in 1888, Hotel del Coronado became the first beach resort on the West Coast. Who has stayed here? Presidents, athletes, and movie stars. Some people even say the hotel has its very own ghost!

he knows very well!

He dives into dinner.
Then what does he find?
Larry is leaving
his family behind!

Poor Larry gets worried.
He leaps from the boat,
and soon he is met
by a girl who can float.

Mission Beach

She gathers up Larry
and brings him to shore.
But this beach is nowhere
he's been to before.

With fast, noisy rides
and an ocean breeze blowing—
a fun place to be,
but he's got to get going.

This world looks like someplace
where fish like to play—
an ocean adventure—
but Larry can't stay.

He jumps in a truck,
and it takes him away!

MISSION BASILICA SAN DIEGO DE ALCALÁ
California was still a Spanish territory when
this Franciscan mission, California's first, was
founded in 1769.

They come to a stop.
Larry leaps from the truck.
Is Pete in this garden?
He might be in luck.

There's a building with bells,
and a flower-filled lane.
But no sign of Pete,
so he hops on a train.

Larry reaches a place
where he's met face-to-face
with pink-feathered birds,
a cat too big to chase,

San Diego Zoo

and odd-looking animals
funny and furry.
But Pete isn't here,
so he leaves in a hurry.

Will these two help Larry?
He hopes that they will.
But while Larry waits,
they stay perfectly still.

El Cid Campeador by Anna Hyatt Huntington

Botanical Building

He stops at a pond
and sees fish swimming in it.
He stays there to watch them,
but just for a minute.

Lily Pond

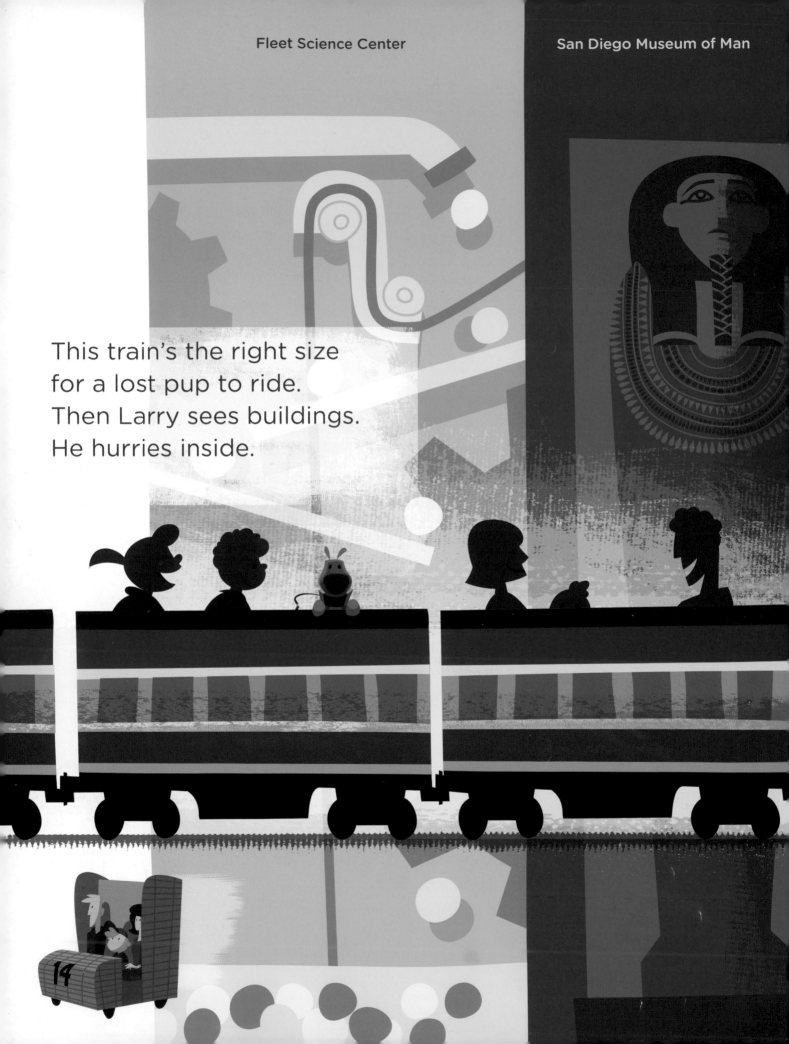

Fleet Science Center

San Diego Museum of Man

This train's the right size
for a lost pup to ride.
Then Larry sees buildings.
He hurries inside.

14

San Diego Natural History Museum

San Diego Model Railroad Museum

There's so much to look at—
things fun, strange, and scary,
and trains that are even
too tiny for Larry.

BALBOA PARK MINIATURE RAILROAD
All aboard! People from around the world have
ridden this miniature train on its three-minute,
half-mile ride through parts of Balboa Park.

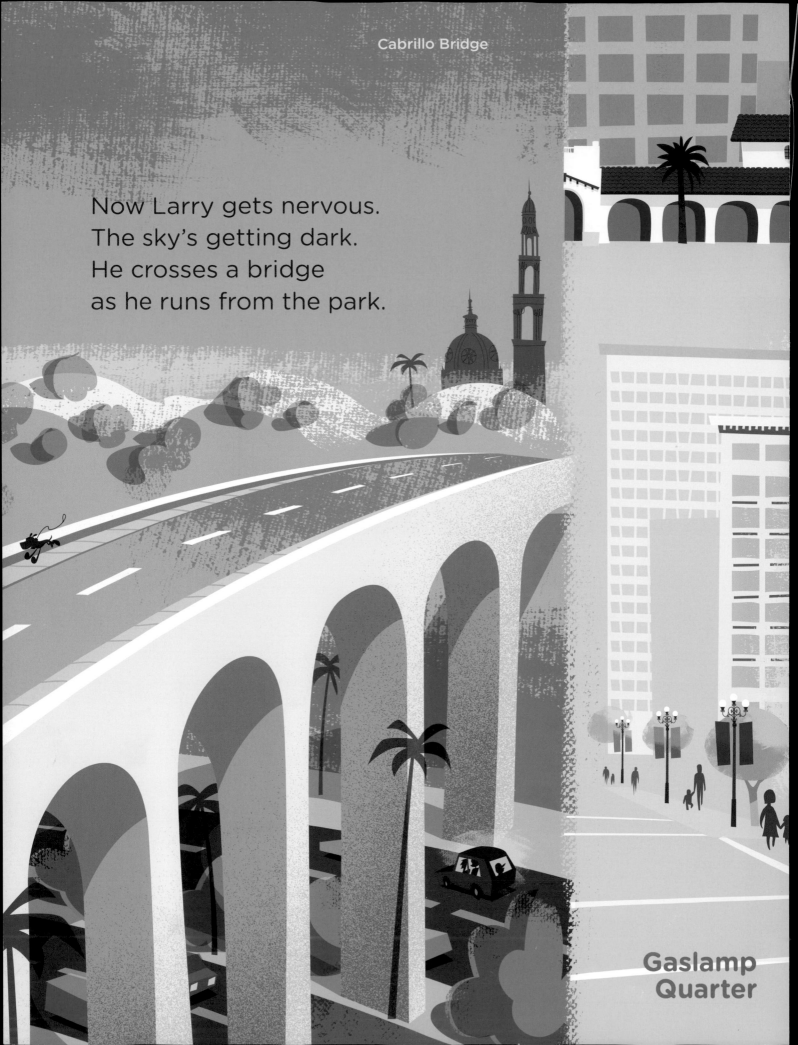

Cabrillo Bridge

Now Larry gets nervous.
The sky's getting dark.
He crosses a bridge
as he runs from the park.

Gaslamp
Quarter

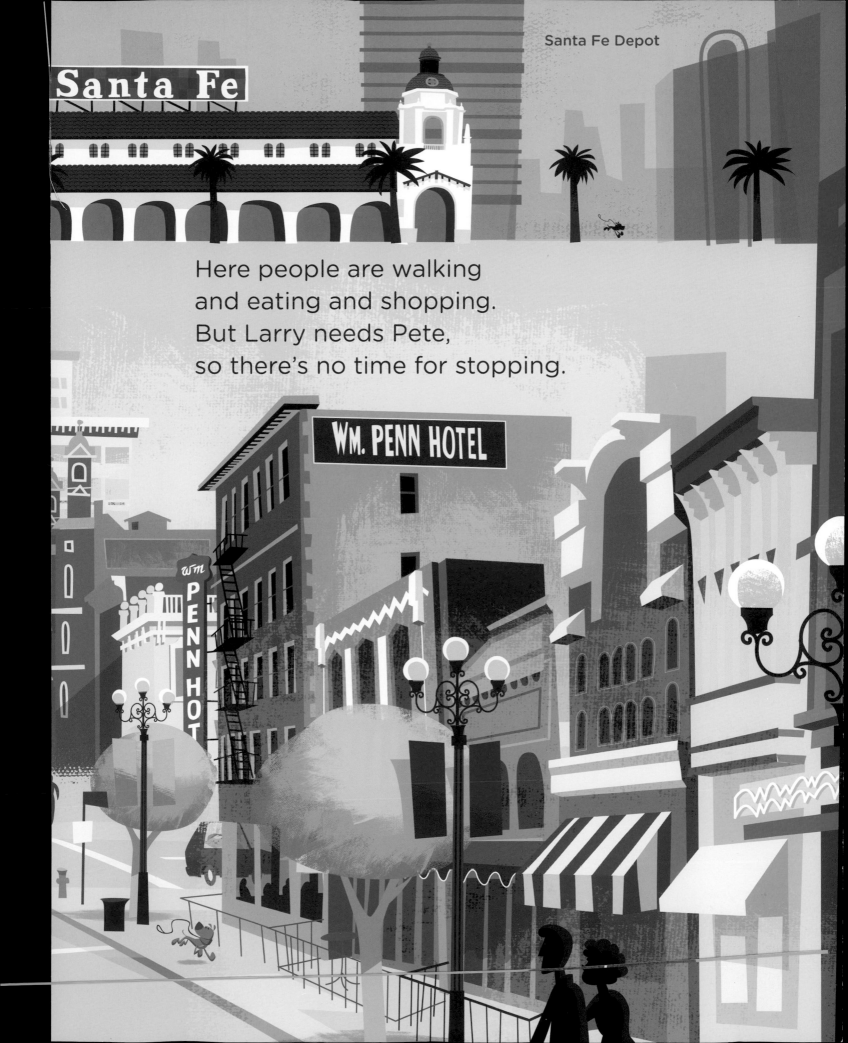

Here people are walking
and eating and shopping.
But Larry needs Pete,
so there's no time for stopping.

PETCO PARK
As home to the San Diego Padres, Petco Park might be best known for Major League Baseball, but the stadium is also used for golf, rugby, and even rock concerts.

He runs past a building
so big and so loud
where Larry hears cheers
from a large, happy crowd.

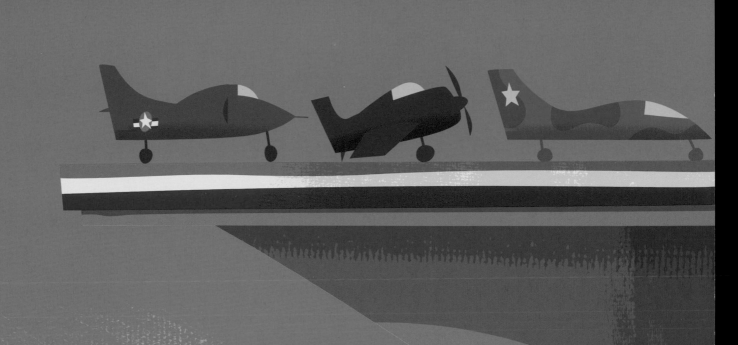

And next there's a ship.
Larry comes to a stop.
It's as big as a city
with planes up on top.

USS *MIDWAY*
Ahoy! One of America's longest-
serving aircraft carriers is now a
floating museum. Guests can explore
more than sixty exhibits and dozens
of restored aircraft.

And these ships look older.
They're proud as you please,
with poles standing straight
and as tall as the trees.

But Larry has no time
for sailing the seas.

MARITIME MU

EMBARCADERO

Where can you see historic ships, visit museums and restaurants, and take a tour of the harbor? San Diego's Embarcadero! *Embarcadero* means "wharf" or "pier" in Spanish.

Shelter Island

Pacific Portal by
James T. Hubbell

He soon finds a ship
that has never set sail
and runs to a man
with a wag of his tail.

RECRUIT

"Ahoy!" shouts the man.
"You should not be alone."
He checks Larry's collar,
then takes out his phone.

USS RECRUIT

USS *Recruit* was designed as a school for US
Navy sailors, but the sailors liked to call the
ship the "USS *Neversail*." Why? Because it has
no engine and has never been on the water.

And soon they're together,
the dog and the boy.
They hug, and they dance,
and they holler with joy.

**JUAN RODRÍGUEZ
CABRILLO STATUE**
This fourteen-foot
statue of Cabrillo by
Álvaro de Brée looks
out over the San Diego
Bay. It's believed the
explorer was the first
European to sail and
chart this coastline.

OLD POINT LOMA LIGHTHOUSE

When this lighthouse was first lit in 1855, sailors realized it was too high above sea level. Low clouds often hid the light. A new one was built closer to the water, and the old lighthouse became a museum.

Then, as the sun sets
and it colors the skies,
they crawl in the car,
and they soon close their eyes.

They dream of the city,
the ships, and the shore—

friends through and through,
and together once more.

Get More Out of This Book

Spooky!

Do you believe in ghosts? If they really exist in the Hotel del Coronado, what might the ghosts' point of view be of the people who have been coming and going from this hotel for almost 130 years? Do you think it is a good thing for a building to have its own ghosts? Would you like to stay in a place that is famous for its own ghosts?

Connect Those Words!

Compound words are easy to spot! Just look for a two-syllable word that has two words put together. Some compound words in this book are "something," "seawall," "lighthouse," "sailboat," "nowhere," "railroad," "baseball," "aircraft," and "coastline." Can you find more?

How Do Legos Work?

Larry and Pete visit Legoland where more than fifty-seven million pieces of Legos were used to build twenty-two thousand sculptures. But how do they fit together? Fractions can explain the phenomenon. A Lego piece is built a fraction of an inch smaller on the top than the bottom so pieces can stick together tight enough to be stacked yet loose enough to be taken apart. The next time you play with Legos, look closely at how the top and bottom are constructed, and experiment with building your own sculpture.

TEACHER'S GUIDE: The above discussion questions and activities tie into our teacher's guide, which is aligned to the Common Core Standards for English Language Arts for Grades K to 1. For the complete guide and a list of the exact standards it aligns with, visit our website: SasquatchBooks.com